CW01507963

Written by: Ash Ericmore

Copyright © 2023 Ash Ericmore

ISBN: 9798388757364

DEVOTEE

EXTREME HORROR

ASH ERICMORE

WITH SPECIAL THANKS TO

CHRISTINA PFEIFFER, LEEANNE WRIGHT, AUGUST VAUGHN, JESSICA SHELLY, DONNA LATHAM, CHRISTOPHER RIDGE, BAMEBALLS, EDDIE GREENHAM, AND TIA WRIGHT

Want to see your name here? Check out

ko-fi.com/ashericmore/tiers

to find out how, as well as see all the other benefits of joining up.

DEVOTEE

CHAPTER 1

Charles looked down at his legs, lounging back in his gaming chair, his computer playing a video of a young woman. He wiggled them back and forth and smiled, a little giggle escaping his mouth. Then he slammed his thumb down on the keyboard and paused it. Getting from the chair, slipping his bare feet into his slippers, he padded slowly to the door of the bedroom. He stood and listened for a moment. The building was quiet. His neighbours must be out. Dragging the bathrobe from the back of the door, he went down the hall to the kitchen and in. Put the kettle on.

It was cold everywhere else in the flat. Just the bedroom. Warm. He looked at the boiler, hoping it wouldn't fire. He looked with a little suspicion at the kettle. The crackle of the heating pad on the bottom of it, the irritation of the water starting. A quick look through the partially shut blinds into the back garden of the house. It was communal so a) no one ever used it, and b) it was overgrown to fuck. Which suited him just fine, because it gave him a little more privacy, what with him having the ground floor flat.

He turned out the kitchen and padded along to the bathroom. There was the odour of bleach in there. Not something he relished, but at least it was *clinically* clean. Dropping the robe from his shoulders he stood, naked apart from his slippers, and slid his hand into the shower. Turned the water on. His cold fingers absently stroked around his ballsack as stood there. Staring at the tiles. Doing nothing. Thinking nothing. Then his other hand went under the water. Then he stepped in.

Head straight under. The violence of the water on his head. He pushed his fingers through it, getting it wet before standing straight and pouring some shampoo into his palm, and rubbing it into his hair.

Then a quick trip around his junk with some body wash.

Turned the shower off, out. Robe on. Back to the kitchen. Poured the coffee into a mug. Blew on it. Another glance out the window.

Back to the bedroom.

The warm.

He slumped down in front of the computer. Left his dressing gown on this time. Noted that it was Thursday. Had to sign on, on Friday. Depressing place, the Job Centre. Full of security guards all looking at you like you'd done something. He sighed. Opened his email. Looked down the list. There were a couple from his advisor telling him he had to attend such and such an event or whatever, and that he was going to start to see repercussions soon enough if he wasn't actively looking for work.

Shaking his head, he opened Facebook. Looked down it. Quickly. He was becoming more detached from the people on there. They weren't *real*. They didn't care about him. It was all some show, apparently for *other* people.

Not for him. Never for him.

He frowned, closed it. Opened Youtube and started watching a movie review for a film he'd seen a thousand times. Drank his coffee. Looked at his phone. He couldn't just sit there all day. He had to go and see his old man. He'd be expecting him.

Coffee in the middle of the morning, and one of those shit cakes from the all night garage.

Charles watched the video.

Morosely.

The wind cut through the clothing he had so carefully selected as if he were wearing fucking shorts. He stepped down to the path, a quick look back to the house. You know, the *did I leave the front door open* look, then he schlumped off towards his father's house.

A ten minute walk.

He had tried to look … half-decent. He would have rather just pulled on anything to go up there and see him. It wasn't like he needed to make an impression was it? The old man already thought he was a waste of space. But, after he was done there, he was going into the town, and he wanted to look good enough for that.

He climbed the hill by the school for the deaf, to the shop at the top, the one next to the church, ducking in for a chocolate bar for later, and then out, along towards the old man's.

The house was a semi-detached. It was the house he'd grown up in. Beaten up old car in the driveway, one that the old man worked on constantly, although, Charles couldn't remember the last time it had moved. He went to the front door and let himself in. Rung the bell as an announcement.

He stood there on the mat for a moment. Waiting for the old man to acknowledge him. It didn't come.

There was the flash in his head that maybe he was dead. Laying in the bed upstairs, breathed his last in the middle of the night. Then he saw the shed door open, looking through from the hallway to the kitchen, out the window to the immaculate back garden. The old man came from the shed. He was wearing coveralls and a flat cap. Looked like an extra from Last of the Summer Wine. He looked through to Charles, the two of them met eyes for a second, and then the look broke. His dad ambled around in the garden, moving generally in the direction of the house. His look didn't change when he saw Charles. He just saw him. Nothing more. Came in the back door, and put the blades of the lawnmower on the side of the sink. Mud dropped from them to the chrome.

"What you doing?" Charles asked.

The old man looked out the window, rather than at Charles. "Aye?" he said. It seemed to be how half of his sentences started these day. "I was cutting the grass, and the mower packed up."

Charles looked at the blades. Why they had been removed was a mystery, and if today went like last Thursday, would likely remain so. "Bit cold for that," he said.

The old man ignored him. "Drink?" He turned and finally looked at him. Looked him down. Didn't say anything derogatory, or anything else. And then looked expectant.

"Coffee, please." Charles smiled at him.

The old man filled the kettle and got the mugs down. Nothing to say. He was focussing on the task in hand, while Charles removed his coat and dropped it at the bottom of the stairs next to the bookcase that still had cookery books on there from before Mum …

Then he went through to the living room. Sat on the two seater. Dad would sit in his chair. Like he had done for as long as Charles could remember. He stared through the blinds, open at the living room window, out to the main road, until the old man brought a tray. He put Charles's coffee down next to him. "Biscuit?" he asked.

Charles shook his head, "No, thank you."

The old man sat. "So, anything on the work front?"

Charles shook his head, again. "There's not much out there at the moment." He kept his eyes from his father, knowing he would know the truth if he looked at him. He always had been able to.

The old man stuffed a biscuit in his mouth. Didn't dip it in his coffee. That was something Mum would do.

Charles took a sip of the coffee. White, no sugar. Close to how he wanted it. He'd had it the same since he was like, fifteen, but he no longer expected the old man to remember. He didn't remember much these days. He was still full of intentions, but the will just wasn't what it was. Charles would return next week, and the old lawnmower would be in the shed, waiting to go down the tip. The blades on top of it. A new mower there next to it.

But the old man was old fashioned. He somehow still remembered that Charles was unemployed, and that made him a fucking bum. Not that he would use that term.

His father never swore.

He slowly nodded his head, his thought

apparently more with the biscuit that anything else. "Hm," he said. Apparently agreeing. "You okay for money?"

"Fine," Charles said. *No. Of course not.* He could barely afford food. But he couldn't say that. And besides, if he tried really hard, or even perhaps just a little, he might be able to get a job. He slurped back some more of his coffee. Bitter. Cheap too. That was a fixed rule in the house. Cheap, instant coffee. Charles sighed. He didn't mean to, but it brought the attention of his father.

"Spoken to your brother?"

"Not this week." Hadn't for weeks, but he didn't need to know that. Andy was the good son. Married. Job. Kid on the way. Sure to be two point four children soon enough. Probably a dog or a hamster or some shit.

Charles knocked back the rest of the coffee. Bit hot for it, but that was it. Time up. Time to get out.

He pushed himself to stand. "Right."

"You off?" The old man looked up at him. There was a look there, somewhere far behind the eyes that looked like disappointment.

Probably, Charles thought, *in him.* "Yeah, things to do."

"Going shopping?" The old man didn't rise from the seat.

Charles didn't blame him. Good. Sit there. Relax for Christ's sake. You're seventy. "Yeah," he said. "Going into town."

A half-truth. He *was* going into town, but he *wasn't* going shopping.

Sitting on the bench outside the library, Charles snacked on the chocolate bar he'd bought earlier. He chewed it thoughtfully, hunched over forward. Made him look like he was a big coat, and not a lot else. Stuffed the chocolate bar in his mouth. Bit off more. Buttery nuts and caramel. Fixed most things. He watched the buses pull up and drop off, pick up, pull away. Busy.

Waiting.

The bus stops outside the library were always busy. A sort of central hub in the town. Over the road, there was a small, expensive, car park. Private dental practice. A bank, long closed. A kebab shop. Fancy one. A Greek restaurant if you will. He gave a glance to a woman fussing over a kid. The kid was in a school uniform. Should have been at school. He wondered if the two of them had come from the dental practice, then dismissed the notion, because if you had private dental, then you didn't take the bus.

There was a community building. One where you could go for advice and courses and that sort of thing. That's what he was looking at.

Waiting.

This time. Every week for the last three weeks.

He pulled his phone and looked the time. The eleven fifty nine from Birchingate would be along shortly. Just after that.

Soon enough, the bus pulled up. People got off. No one got on. The bus changed its destination sign, back to Birchingate and then pulled out, empty. No one apparently wanting to go to Birchingate. Not really a surprise. Charles had been there a few times.

It wasn't the best place in the world.

As the bus cranked itself back out into the traffic, Charles watched as the community hub doors opened. A few people coming out. Twelve o'clock. Morning turn out.

He watched as Lauren Corbin came out. She was smiling. Her smile lit up the street. It always did. Always had. Ever since Charles was at school. They'd been in the same physics class. He'd always wished he'd asked her out. Back then. But he didn't have the balls. She was perfect. Always had been. Always would be.

He pushed the remainder of the chocolate bar in his mouth. Watching her go over to the car in the car park. Waiting for her. Like it always was. Like royalty. Her driver, whatever. She opened the car door, brushing away help from anyone, and slumped herself in there. Pulling the crutches in after her.

Shutting the door.

The smile never wavering.

CHAPTER 2

Charles trudged back along from the town centre to the flats and in. Pushing his front door open, even though he had no heating in there, he could still feel the warmth of the place. Kicked his shoes off and dropped his coat down by the front door. The air felt like snow was coming. You know that feeling, like a freshness. Maybe it was just because of where he lived, near the seaside. Maybe that was why the air felt different. There was probably some scientific name for it, two weather fronts clashing over the cliffs.

He shook his head. Found himself in the kitchen, looking out through the overgrowth. One of the neighbours was in the back garden. She was in a bathrobe or a dressing gown or something. Tossing nuts into the grass in the middle of it all. She lived in the basement. She'd said her name once when they bumped into each other when he moved in, but he never caught it and didn't want to ask again. There was a guy called Soldad or something living upstairs. He was quiet, and that was pretty much all that mattered.

What's-her-name wrapped her arms around herself, cuddling herself, a look up to the sky. Clearly she thought something was up with the weather too. Charles thought that she must work nights or something. He rarely heard anything from her, and it was the middle of the day and she was in a gown. She looked like she had just gotten up.

He opened the fridge and looked in it. Closed the

door.

To the bedroom. He pulled the computer chair out and sat on it, legs across the edge of the desk. Leaning back. He opened Youtube and pulled up the one person he was subscribed to.

Lauren Corbin.

He selected the most popular video from the *Most Popular* playlist and pressed play. Laying back in the chair and closing his eyes. He'd seen it innumerable times. Didn't need to see it again. It was from about a year ago. She was doing something new to the channel. It had obviously worked, what with it being the most viewed video on the channel. He listened as she walked through the forest on the screen.

He knew the forest. Eventually. It had taken him a while to work it out, of course. She was in the small woods on the outskirts of Ashbury—the city around twenty miles away. She was talking, it was a summer's day. She talked about what she was doing for a living and how much she enjoyed it, but how her videos were doing well, and how she liked doing them so much more. But he was getting ahead of himself. She wasn't talking about that yet. That was later. At the moment, she was walking under the trees, cooing over the niceness of it all. The shards of light spearing, heavy as they cut through the greenery, flashing across her skin. Bronzing it, from the bull grey of the shade, making it *live*. The sound of her feet in the leaves, fallen from the year before.

Her voice was low, and subtle. That was why the channel did so well. But these video logs that she had started, they were super popular. Cataloguing her every move. Well, curated as it was. In the video at the end, she got back to the car park, and that was how Charles had managed to find the right patch of forestry. From the flash of the car park, by pausing it just at the right time. Between that, and some of the vocal clues about it not being far from home, and of course, Google maps.

He'd even been out there once. Trodden the same path, as best he could. There were no leaves though, so it wasn't the same.

He opened his eyes and looked at the video. She turned the camera on her face. The only time in the video that she did. A smile into it. She didn't have much makeup on. She did in some of the videos. The other ones. But rarely in the log videos. Like she was acting in the other videos and this was *really* her.

Like when they were at school.

He smiled back at the vision of her, and then closed his eyes again listening to her real voice. He liked her real voice. It had this air of innocence about it.

This child-like quality. Like he remembered.

The crunching of her feet stopped, and she was back at the car park. She said that she hoped everyone enjoyed walking with her. There was that flash of the car park, then the video ended.

Charles sat there unmoving.

Listening to the silence in the flat.

Then the next video autoplayed. It was a random selection, so not always going to the same video. He knew which one it was though. It was a good one. She whispered. "Hi. Are you ready?"

There was a pause for a response.

Then she asked, hushed in a whisper, "How does

this make you feel?"

The sound of her licking something filled the room.

"Oh, God," Charles muttered. He was getting hard in his jeans.

The sound of tongue on ear. She was licking something shaped like an ear. He'd watched her do it many times. The sound from the speaker, loud. It was better with headphones on, but he didn't know this video was going to play. His fingers squirmed around his fly. He couldn't help himself. He couldn't *not*. Fly open. Fingers in.

"Lauren," he whispered back.

"Come on," she whispered. "For me."

Charles got his cock out, and started to slowly jerk it. In time with the licks. The goads. The whispers. Listening. Falling into it. Surrounded by her. Encompassed by her.

He sighed, getting closer to the edge. Then he stopped. Opened his eyes. He reached forward with his fingers, sticky with clear liquid, trickling from his head. Stroked the side of her face as she looked into the camera. Into him. His soul. Then he lie back. Carrying on. Knowing what she looked like for the rest of the video.

Seeing if he could make it to the end this time.

He never had yet.

CHAPTER 3

"It's like the fucking dark side of the moon." Ben kicked back, his feet up on the stool in front of him. His eyes never leaving the TV.

Charles looked at him. "I don't get it."

"The internet," said Neet. "Everything has a dark side."

"Well, yeah." Charles pushed himself up and looked between the two of them. He knew Ben from his last job, although they'd been at school together—well, Ben had been a year older than Charles—and Neet was Ben's girlfriend. They'd just moved in together. Poxy small two up, two down. Bought it.

Fuckers.

Whatever.

"But what do you mean *in particular?*" Charles continued.

"Anything," Ben said. He was holding a beer on his belly. His focus almost entirely on the TV. Some horror film.

One that Charles had all but forgotten about. Charles, sitting forward on the sofa, next to Neet, like he was about to get up and go. He turned, clearly going to get nothing from Ben, and focussed on her instead. He could get in her line of sight better. "What does he mean?"

She looked from the film to him. "Look," she said. "We just think you've been spending too much time doing nothing, and maybe you should get another job."

That was clearly what *she* thought. Ben didn't think that. Ben was his real friend. "Right. But what about the internet?"

"You're defending it like it's your friend."

It was. Clearly the only one he had. He glanced down Neet. She was a pretty girl, but too thin. Probably too good for Ben too. She was training to be a school teacher, and he had a dead end job in the bank in town. "I just don't think there's anything wrong with it." He turned his attention back to the TV. Watch the film. Shut them up. Drink their beer. Didn't have any at home, or he might have gone. That would show them.

Neet sighed. "We just want what's best for you."

Yeah. Sure. "Okay," Charles said, quietly. That was his signal. Convo over. Some scream queen was getting butchered in the film. Good.

The rest of the film played out with none of them talking until the credits ran. Ben turned and looked at him. He smiled. "You just always seem to have something to say about it. That's all."

Picking the conversation up from where it had been left off.

"And I'd rather see you doing something than nothing. You keep talking about …" he stopped and looked at his beer. A glance to Neet. "You know what? Never mind."

Charles slipped his beer bottle on the coffee table, and Neet immediately picked it up and put it on a coaster. "So how's work been?" he said.

Neet stood. "I'm gonna turn in."

Oh. It was like that. Charles stood. "I'll be off

then."

She just turned away and went off. Not even a goodnight. Charles watched her go. Then he noticed that Ben was watching him watching her. But it wasn't *like that*.

"You meet anyone recently?" he asked.

Charles shook his head. "There's a sort of someone."

"Real?" He grinned like people on the internet weren't real.

"Real," Charles confirmed. Just because they hadn't spoken in years, and that she might not even remember him didn't make her any less *real*.

"Seeing her?" he asked. He still hadn't moved from his seat, and Charles was still standing awkwardly. Gangly.

"No."

Ben nodded. Pushed himself up from the chair. "I will see you anon, then." He grinned. Bit pissed up, Charles thought.

"Anon," he echoed.

Ben crossed the front of him and went to the hallway, getting his coat. The two of them made some uncomfortable bro sounds at each other, and Charles was still pulling his coat on when Ben closed the front door, leaving him in the cul-de-sac, alone. Middle of the night.

One town over.

He hoofed it to the end of the street and into the street lights. Who the fuck buys a house in a road with no street lights? In a town like this? This place was even worse than where he lived. No seaside here, one town over. Just rot and decay. Last week some geezer got airlifted to hospital after being stabbed up in the main drag, just around the corner from where he stood.

Charles walked along under the street lights to the end of the road, and around the corner. Down the hill. There was someone walking towards him, but she looked more scared than him, so he didn't worry too much about her trying to rob him. He even stepped from the path into the road, to give her enough space. Try to make her feel a little better about him.

He glanced at her, just as they passed and their eyes met and Charles hated himself for a second because she probably thought he was a creeper or some shit, but that disappeared quickly. Probably the beer.

And he needed to pee.

Already. Fucking hell. It was at least forty minutes to walk home, and that was if he went straight. Which he wasn't. Through the traffic lights at the bottom of the hill. He looked into the window of the fish and chip shop that was open late, through the heavy condensation on the inside. Park on the other side of the road. Small one. Had a toilet block—which was locked, although Charles didn't want to get raped and beaten to death in a toilet block, so wouldn't have gone in anyway—and was the perfect building to go behind and pee, but you know, *raped and beaten to death*.

Top of the next hill. Burning in the bladder. Had to pee now.

Charles left the path, and went into someone's front garden. Lights all out. He pissed into the bush, hidden from the road. It didn't want to come out. Stage fright. A bit of dribble before and after, and probably on his trousers, but no one was going to see. Not at that time.

Then he carried on, along the road. Main road. Lot of houses. There was a pub turning out. He ignored the jeers and shit from the slashed up punters. If you don't acknowledge them, they're less likely to stab you. At least, that was the theory. Then to the left. Follow the road up towards the railway station.

Big houses. Nice ones.

Just off the bus route, too. Near the train station. Plusses all around.

Charles looked at the houses on the left, as he walked on the right. Some money in those things. Then he turned a hard right into a driveway. The car that had picked her up earlier there, in the driveway. He ran his finger down the paintwork. Clean. A glance in the window to the immaculately valeted vehicle. He stopped, looked around quickly. The front of the house was shrouded in darkness as he knew it would be, but he wanted to make sure he was alone in the street, and then he hopped up onto the wall, and stepped over the gate to the sideway. Behind the gate, he used the top of the bin to steady himself, then he dropped down into the darkness.

In the sheer black he went up the side of the house, stepping around the pile of flowerpots that he couldn't see. They were always there. Then onto the grass. He went to the end of the garden, the picnic table, where he sat, back to the table looking at the house.

The light was on in the window, top right. Thin

pink curtains. The occasional shadow playing in the light. He watched, feeling close to her. Hood up. It was getting colder. Sometimes he brought something to eat, you know, once he'd found there was a picnic table there. He could sit and eat with her. Watching the shadows. In the pink room. He knew what the inside of the room looked like because she streamed from there sometimes. More so recently, of course, what with her mobility issues.

His phone vibrated in his pocket. He pulled it and looked at the notification. She'd just uploaded something. Nice. He felt like he was on set. She moved across the light behind the curtains and he almost gave a little wave. Had to stop himself. Pushed his phone back in his pocket. He'd watch whatever that was when he got home.

Charles felt something on his face. He reached up and wiped it away. It was a splotch of sleet. Great. It *was* getting cold. He looked up into the black sky. There were small blobs of it dropping. He looked at the darkness of the grass. Couldn't tell if it was laying. Shit. *Laying*. If it laid, he couldn't be there. He'd leave footprints. If she thought someone was in, or had been in, her back garden she might put up cameras, or spot lights, or something. That would spoil everything.

He pushed himself up to stand. Looked like the video she'd just uploaded was going to have to be enough. He hurried through the darkness to the sideway. Kicked the flowerpots. "Shit," he hissed, stopping. Still as the night itself. He waited.

And waited.

When nothing happened, he crouched down and pushed them back to where they should have been, almost blind in the black. Then up. On the bin. A quick check of the still street, and over.

Once on the path he pulled the phone, thumbing it as he walked in the direction of the station. The video she had uploaded was a log. Good. It would be nice to see how she was doing. He flipped over to his email. Nothing new in the last hour or so, not except spam.

He turned at the station and headed down the hill, towards the traffic lights.

Then on, home.

CHAPTER 4

Opening the door to the flat, Charles kicked his shoes off. Shook his coat down his shoulders. His fingers numb with cold. It had snowed pretty hard. Laying too. Which was bullshit he didn't need to deal with. Put a crimp on his night time activities. He went to the bedroom and flipped the power to his computer on. He pulled his dressing gown on over his clothes. Could see his breath even inside the flat. He turned on the heater at his feet, ignoring the central heating. Get a little warmth in the room.

Slumped down in the chair, he opened his browser, and waited for the thing to sort itself out. He wanted to wait until he was warm before he watched Lauren's video. He wanted that to be the last thing he watched. So he opened Porn Hub and started to browse. Nothing really in particular he wanted. He looked at the popular videos on the home page. All the same stuff as usual. Opened the menu, went down a couple of the categories.

Nothing immediately struck him.

He closed the window. The fan heater filling the room with stuffy air, smelling of burned dust, in seconds. He pulled his trousers off, under the robe, unwilling to discard the heat from it, but wanting his legs free.

Then he sat, and opened the log from Lauren. She was sitting on the bed. In the pink room. Smiling into the camera. There was something different about her smile these days. She was holding back her emotion—smiling *just* for the camera, if you will. It didn't make Charles feel particularly good. He could put a real smile on her face. He knew he could. She suddenly sat back and began speaking. The usual benign pleasantries from the start of one of these videos. *Hey*'s and *how you doing*'s, before she dove right in and said what she wanted. The camera was on a tripod facing her, so she could get away from it. Show more of herself. She was talking about her recent changes and how she was adapting. How everything was new, and exciting.

She didn't sound like things were either new, nor exciting.

She showed her stump to the camera. She said she hated the way it looked, but the outpouring of sympathy in the comments had been heart-warming, and by having it out, here with her, was helping her to get used to it, and not see it as an obstacle. She was going to start doing the sensory response videos again soon enough, but she hadn't felt like doing them. Not recently.

Then she started talking about how she was going to move forward, some with the channel, other bits about her leg, and new aids she was going to be buying. Charles opened the draw of the desk and pulled out a craft knife. Extended the blade and then slipped it onto the desk. He kicked back. His feet up on the edge of the desk, he pulled his dressing gown open. Ran his cold fingers down his flesh. Goosebumps rising. His hair sticking up. He took the knife, and with the other hand caressed himself just above the knee. His eyes on her. Looking at her leg, her stump. His cock twitched.

Couldn't help it.

He scraped the knife over the hair, slipping the

new blade through it, shaving himself carefully. Eyes on that. He didn't want to cut himself. Then he rested the blade down. His fingers were shaking lightly. Might be the cold. He sat back and looked at her. Watched her intently. His gaze jumping from her eyes, full of deceit, to her stump. Her finger slipping over it like she was massaging away some pain.

He did the same to his leg, his eyes not leaving her, running his fingers over the flesh. Breathing becoming harder. He could feel his heart beating in his chest.

She smiled at the camera, this time a little more warmly, like she was getting used to the camera being on her leg. But he'd seen her acting like it before. She always felt somewhat better the longer the video went on, like the camera was hugging her, and making her feel as warm as it did to him. He glanced to the blade and then his leg. He was hard in his boxers, just from that. He thought about waiting for the video to finish, and then putting on one of her earlier videos. Release that way.

But he didn't. He watched her say good night. Then the video ended. Charles stopped it from loading the next one. He took the knife and held it on his skin. Just above the knee. Could feel the cold sting of the metal on his leg. A smile. He pushed it into the skin. Down, straight, and deep enough. He'd learned quickly that light slashes just stung hard. Like fucking paper-cuts on the skin, dipped in lemon. If he pushed the blade into the flesh, down then the pain was real, and there was no *sting*. He sucked air in, through his teeth, the pain blooming from the wound as he held it there.

He was careful to stay away from the muscles, so

he didn't limp the next day, as well as the major arteries. He had no real desire to bleed out there in his bedroom, feet on the desk. Not really.

Not at the moment, anyway.

Charles pulled the blade out, carefully, straight upwards, so as not to make the wound worse. Blood drooled from the cut, over his leg, down, into the fabric of the dressing gown. Then he slipped it in again, a few centimetres from the first. Down again. The same depth. The warmth of the pain surrounding him. Just like the camera, her. He looked at his toes and wiggled them. The movement encouraging more blood from the cut. He pulled the knife again and looked at the smears on it. He retracted the blade. Tossed it aside. He looked around the floor and picked up a t-shirt. Black one. It would do. Then he wrapped it around the two inch-long cuts in his leg. Going to the bed.

He lay.

Ignoring the ache in his groin. That would have to wait for a while. Instead, he closed his eyes. Listening to the fan heater whirring, thinking of her. Her face. Her stump. Her voice.

Her perfection.

CHAPTER 5

Charles stared down at the blood on the bed. Oh well. He pulled the covers over it and ignored it. It didn't matter. No one was going to see them were they? He sighed. He'd fallen asleep like that.

Slept well, too.

Of course. With the heater on. And the lights. And the computer. All of which were off now. He went to the light switch and flicked it on and off. Nothing. He'd left everything going and run down his pre-payment meter. He went to the meter in the hallway, and crouched down, looking at it. Just to prove it to himself. Yep. Zero fucking electric. He shook himself, trying to muster some blood flow in his limbs, as he wrapped his gown around him. Looked at the charge on his phone. He had fifty percent. Fine that would last him the day. Charles went to the kitchen. Stared at the kitchen, the useless kettle. The fridge that wasn't running. Said fuck. Then went back to the bedroom and changed. Put clothes on to stay warm.

Back to the kitchen.

He grabbed the card for the meter from the drawer, and looked longingly at the kettle. Balls. He stuffed the card in his wallet, noting of course the distinct lack of funds in there. Then he went out. Saw the woman from downstairs, just coming in. The two of them grunted some half-arsed greeting as they walked by each other. He hunched himself up and walked to the centre. The snow wasn't deep enough to be snow-snow. It was that shit brown slush shit that then precluded any further snowfall from laying, and guaranteeing that all snow from this point forward was going to deepen said slush shit.

He stomped through it.

Glad to have two legs right then.

To the centre. To the cash point. He pushed his card in and looked at his balance. Well. That was as close to zero as it mattered. He couldn't get anything smaller than a ten out the machine—not that you could put less than ten on an electric card.

He stared at the little screen for a moment, before cancelling his way back to getting his card in his hand again, then he pushed that back in his wallet, taking off across the square and into the high street. He looked at the doorways of the empty shops. Somewhere he could sit, and beg. That was something to try. Maybe.

He was walking up the high street—with no particular direction in his head—but his muscle memory seemed to be aiming him at his old man's place. Go home and ask to borrow money. Home. He snorted, his nose cold and runny. Hadn't thought about it like that for some … years.

He turned, walking up the covered section, getting out the light sleet, behind the shops, up, across the front of the café. There was a homeless guy sitting on the benches there. The woman who worked the front of the café was staring out the window at him. The rest of the café was empty. She looked forlorn. Like this homeless guy was chasing away their custom. Not the Greek place that had just opened around the corner.

Charles carried on, though. Ignoring all of it. A

woman cut across the front of him, coming from the direction of the multi-storey car park. Hurrying, almost a run. High heels in slush. She was going to do herself a mischief if she wasn't careful. Charles just stood there for a moment.

Watching the people coming and going.

One catching his eye. A young woman. Reminded him of … he looked down her, as she strode purposefully across the pedestrian area, back towards the council offices. Her legs. Long and slender. She wasn't wearing any tights or stockings. He could see her flesh, goosebumped in the cold. Needing to be warmed.

Charles turned on his heels and followed her.

Watching her feet. Her legs. As she turned, again, surprising him. Down the side of the old bank.

He looked up at the sky. The clouds deep and purple. It looked like there was going to be a hard snowstorm. Unusual for the area. His eyes dropped from the sky to the back of her. Walking towards the toilet block.

She obviously wasn't going to the council offices. Otherwise she'd go in there. Nobody used the public toilets down there. They stank. They weren't safe. Used mostly in the early evening for drug deals. He suspected, of course. He knew nothing about that malarkey. Charles followed her as she went to the back of the building and turned into the toilets.

He stopped at the door to the gents. Half listening to see if there was someone in there. Half looking to see if anyone was watching.

Then he continued to the next door and went in. Standing in the tiled corridor, looking at the wall as it ran to the left, and around. He could hear her in there. She sniffed up something, like she was hawking a lougie. But she sounded alone. The door to a cubicle went. Creak to open, knocking sound to close.

No sound of the lock.

Probably didn't have one. These shitters were fucked beyond belief. Charles checked again to make sure there was no one looking, following, then he walked around into the toilets. The opening in the men's side always had rivers of piss on the floor, the doors to the cubicles were graffiti'd in paint and human shit, usually, and there was often some undefinable fluids staining something.

The ladies side wasn't much better.

Less wee on the floor. No urinals.

Not something Charles had really ever considered. Them having no urinals, and a couple more cubicles. Which did mean that men could get through quicker, although, no one wanted to stand next to someone else at a urinal, right? He was staring at the only closed cubicle door. Could hear pissing.

Fucking hell. She was actually using the toilet. He'd just assumed somewhere in the back of his head that she was going to be doing a line of coke or something. She must have really needed to go. Charles brought his foot up and kicked the door of the cubicle in.

The door crashed against her knees as she hovered over the stank hole that passed for a toilet, and spun her around. Skirt half held up, piss spinning everywhere, she crashed to the side of the cubicle, peeing on the floor now, Charles in, fist up. He punched her hard. He wasn't good at robbing people.

Hadn't had to do it much. He contacted with the side of her head, killing the scream almost instantly as she fell back, then sitting on the shitter. Piss hitting water again. She looked stunned. Looked around, rather than at him. Like she couldn't see him. The sound in the toilet silent, apart from her breathing. He brought his fist up again and punched her on the nose this time. Her face split open like ripe fruit, and she crashed backwards. Blood squitting out of her, spraying down her clothes, until it slowed to a dribble. A drool.

Staining her.

Charles was breathing hard. His heart thumping like he'd never felt before. It was the rush. The adrenaline. He looked at the floor. Her bag. He picked it up and jammed his hand in. Grabbed around. Pulled her phone. Tossed it to the side. Smashing it on the hard tiled floor. Even he wasn't desperate enough to try and fence something. He grabbed her wallet. Dropped her bag.

She was looking at him. "Take what you want," she said. She didn't move when she said it. Slumped back on the toilet, the seat broken askew, skirt and panties at her ankles. Blood on her coat. A light coat. She wasn't dressed appropriately. Maybe that was why she needed to pee so badly that she was willing to come in here. That always happened to Charles. Needing to pee when he got cold. But the two of them were now staring at each other. And she wasn't just staring at him.

Charles thought she was *studying* him.

He pushed her wallet into his coat pocket, and stepped into the cubicle with her. She tried to move, realising he wasn't just going to leave, as he kicked the door shut behind him. He raised his fist again, punching her in the face. Could feel the bone in there. Her bone on his. The wind going from her instantly. She didn't even raise a hand in self-defence. Maybe from the shock. Her head banged back against the cistern behind her. The bong of the bone on porcelain echoing around the room.

Charles hit her again. The blood flowing harder and faster. Her nose was a mess on her face by the time he'd hit her a fourth time. He wondered why he had thought she looked like Lauren. A glance down to her legs. Then up, her eyes rolling around in her skull now, like she was a cartoon character. Lost her ability to control her muscles he guessed. It was kinda funny. But he really had no time for that.

He punched her again.

This time her head bounced backwards, but didn't come forward again. Blood spitting up the back of the cubicle like he'd shot her in the face. The back of the toilet doing some of the work for him. He wondered. Just there, in that split second, if it mattered what he did now? She was still breathing, but was she going to recover? Was she going to remember his face? Fuck it—would she even live until someone found her? He took a deep breath. Looked at his hand. Under the blood from her face he could see he'd gashed his skin. Probably on one of her teeth or something.

She shuddered. Charles didn't think it was a voluntary thing. Just a human reaction. Getting colder because there was less blood in her. Her clothes, ruined at the front. That stain was never coming out.

He was shaking. A little.

Then he punched her again. Hard as he could. And again. Her eyes closed, her body wasn't moving. Blood letting down to the tiles on the floor, browned with stains and age, blood tuning them black. He looked in close. Saw she wasn't breathing.

Suddenly shivering. He felt cold. Coming out of the cubicle, Charles pulled the door closed, kicking the broken phone under it, into the blood. He quickly washed her goo from him, and looked at his hand. It was okay. Might need a plaster on it when he got home. He didn't look himself in the mirror. Smeared with something, he didn't want to try and see though the gunk to look himself in the eyes.

If he could bring himself to, anyway.

He looked down his clothes. A couple of blood spots on his coat. You could barely see them, and after he'd been out in the snow, they'd disappear quick enough. He went to the door, back into the street. The sleet had turned to snow. It was weird. Dark because of the cloud cover, but bright, and fresh with the snowfall. He stepped out. There were a couple people running about in the weather. Trying to keep dry or warm or whatever. He just strolled away. No one watched him. No one cared.

He went over to the council offices, and then over the road into the small grass covered square. Empty in the snowfall, getting harder. He followed the path to the centre, to the seating, and sat on a bench. He pulled the woman's wallet from his pocket. His fingers pink. Cold. He took two ten pound notes from inside. Opened the little zipped section on the side and tipped out the coins from in there. A johnny, too. Stuffed it in his pockets, and tossed the wallet in the waste bin.

Then he got up, thrust his hands in his pockets and went to the shop at the end of his road.

Little place. Open like, eighteen hours a day.

He bought ten pounds worth of electricity, one can of cider—the good stuff—, some crisps, and a couple of pots you poured hot water over to make shit dinners. Even got some change from the twenty.

Chapter 6

The fan heater warmed the room quickly, and the computer beeped as it turned on. Charles sat, put the change from his pocket, the change from the twenty, and the johnny on the desk, between him and the keyboard. He counted it out.

Enough for some chips from the chippy, or a day pass on the bus.

He drew air in. *Choices-choices.* A snort of a laugh. He opened a bag of crisps and popped one in his mouth. They weren't proper crisps. They were corn snacks. Good enough, though. He let the thing sit on his tongue, prickling it. Until he could take no more of the feeling of it melting, before he chewed it and swallowed. He pushed himself up and took his coat off now it was warmer.

He checked the front of it. You couldn't see the blood now.

Then he went to the bathroom. While the computer sorted itself out. It was getting old. He knew that, but there was no way he was going to be able to afford a new one.

Charles opened the bathroom cabinet and pulled out a packet of plasters that might have been there since the dawn of time. Honestly, he couldn't remember buying them. Maybe they were in there when he moved in.

Gross.

He pulled the plaster out the little protective sleeve and slapped it across the wound on his hand. It didn't cover it properly, and he wasn't being careful. So he tried a couple more, until his hand looked like he'd stuck duct tape all over it.

But it protected it. He flexed it. Sore. Aches cutting through his bones like he'd been grafting.

He looked in the mirror. Looked at himself. Closed his eyes and saw the woman, her face wrecked. Blood. Gore. Viscera.

Then the vomit came.

He turned, bowing before the toilet as the puke rose acidic inside him. From his gut to his throat. He could taste it, smell it, as it fired from him. Hard and fast. Until he was standing there, over the bowl, puke clinging to him like jelly. Spitting it out, and rinsing his mouth in the sink.

Charles returned to the bedroom. Closed the door to keep the warm in. He sat at the computer. Opened the browser. Opened the cider and sat back. Tasted the drink. The first mouthful washing away the remnant of the puke. The second was nice. Fruity. It was cold on his lips. Didn't warm him. Not physically, but something in that can gave him a hug.

He opened her page. There was a new video. He looked at his phone. There was a notification. He just hadn't heard it.

He played it. Another log by the look of it.

The video panned around to her and she smiled at the camera. There was a pause, like she should have edited this bit out, but had forgotten. She looked down. Away. Thinking. Then back to the camera, and a half-hearted laugh. "I hate this," she said.

Charles watched as she out poured her heart to the camera. The accident only six months ago, the accident that had taken her leg. She wished she could turn back time. Undo it. Start afresh. Then she wouldn't need anyone. She wouldn't need to be driven about. She wouldn't need to rely on other people.

She could be sexy again.

Charles ran his fingers down the image of her, pausing it, when she was full face on the screen. He could see her tears. He could *feel* them. And he could help. She needed to know that she was still sexy, and she could re-gain her independence, or perhaps, rely on someone else for support.

He looked down himself. He was a fucking shambles of a man, but he could love. He could be with her, and they could struggle together. A unionship. Partners. He shook his head, internal grappling with the idea that she could … and they could …

… balance.

He watched the rest of the video in silence. His face too close to the screen.

She said she was still going to try making these videos for as long as she could. But she didn't know how long she would have any desire.

He could help with that too. Before the next video was playing, he was up, hunching over the mouse, stopping the browser. Then pulling his coat on.

He could help her.

CHAPTER 7

Charles walked along the snow-covered path. There had been less footfall there and the snow was fresh to walk on, the crisp crunch of it as his shoes crushed it beneath his feet. He looked at the houses. Only having been there the night before, everything looked so different with only an inch of snow on it. And the fresh fragrance that a layer of snow brought. It was all so clean and nice.

It also brightened the darkness a little too.

He got to the house. A look back down the road behind him. It was brighter, easier for them to see him.

But with no one around, he ducked down the side of the car. Onto the wall. Then over the fence.

Landing in the snow on the other side. Darker, yet still somewhat brighter than before. Charles looked with disdain at the flowerpots. Snorted out a forgiving little grunt and then headed into the garden.

Like a fairy wonderland.

He went, leaving footprints across the grass to the bench, and sat. Looking up to the house for the first time, he saw the light in her room flick off. It was early for her to be turning in. He was hoping for a little alone time before she did. He stared at the blackness of the back of the house a little disappointed, before another light came on.

In the next window. Then one downstairs.

She wasn't turning in. She was on the move.

Charles watched, waiting. The warmth of

imagining her there, going from room to room. A shadow downstairs crossing the window. He wondered how she went down stairs. Did she have a lift or was it a stair lift? She couldn't be fighting her way down them manually.

Then the lights went out again. The back of the house pitched in bleak darkness.

Charles frowned. She couldn't be staying the night downstairs, that would be ridiculous. She must be at the front of the house somewhere. Maybe in the living room, maybe that was at the front. She could be watching TV. Staying up late. He shivered, his hands wrapped around him. He needed to get inside.

Charles got from the bench and walked over to the house. As he got closer, anyone in the windows of the surrounding houses wouldn't see him. Further away, he was in the darkness, so it didn't really matter. He went to the back door and tried the handle.

Locked. That would have been too easy, though, right? He smiled. Of course. He scouted around the windows quickly, making sure that he didn't have an easy way in. Then when he found he didn't, he went to the greenhouse and pulled it open. He hadn't spent a lot of time in people's back gardens at night. Some, but not a lot. But one thing he had found was that people tended to use greenhouses like sheds, but they didn't lock.

He bent down and picked up the dibber. A device used for making holes in the ground to plant seeds. Basically, a foot long metal spike with a handle. He took it, closed the greenhouse up behind him, and went back to the house. Looked around the window next to the back door. The front and back of the house was double-glazed, but the doors were original.

Probably a *feature*. But with that came easier access. Trying to break into a double-glazed door was a no-no. The fucking things had three or four locks stretching the length of them. But these feature wood doors—and in this case, the small window next to it, not double glazed to maintain the 'look'—easy as fuck. He found the widest gap in the window, and pushed the dibber in. Levering it gently towards the house, pulling the window open. The crack of the wood, loud next to his ear in the quiet, golden, silence. He stopped and waited. Listening for movement in the house. Anything to suggest he'd been rumbled.

Once he was satisfied, he pushed again, popping the window forward, the wood splintering quietly. The window, open. He dropped the dibber to the snow and looked through the opening, the warm air flooding out to the cold.

He could smell something. Something floral. A perfume, or something. Her. He was happy that it was the smell of her. He boosted himself up to the window, onto his knees and crawled in through the small gap, slowly. Pain shooting through his joints as he did, but carefully, and slow. Quiet. Moving things out the way instead of pushing them aside. Knowing she was in there somewhere. Hoping the TV was up loud.

He struggled, finally getting himself down, feet firmly on Earth, turning, he closed the window behind him. Didn't close properly. But that didn't matter. He would be staying. He was sure he could fix it in a day or two. When everything was back to normal. She might earn enough from her videos to pay someone else to fix it.

But it would be better if he did it.

Show willing, after all, he was the one that broke it. Show her how helpful he was going to be. How balanced everything was going to be from then on. He smiled to himself. The warmth of the house feeding his internal glow. It was all coming together. He shook his coat off and dropped it behind him. And he stood there. In the hallway. The stair lift rails terminating at the base of the stairs. See. He knew she used something to get down the stairs.

He could hear her. The TV, anyway, in the living room. His eyes accustomed to the dark, he could see light under the door. Charles turned the other way, and went into the kitchen. He looked out the window. The blinds down, but turned open. Snow was coming down harder than when he'd been out there only minutes ago. His footprints dying in the night. Not that it mattered. She'd know he was there in a few minutes anyway.

He twisted the control at the side of the window and closed the blinds. Blocking out the snow. The outside. Then he went to the dining room. The curtains in there already pulled across. He stopped and straightened them. A little peek through. The bite of the cold in his fingers crackling as he warmed.

Then the room doused with light, and the TV was louder.

Charles turned.

There was a man, standing in the doorway to the living room. He was wearing a t-shirt. A pair of sweatpants. He looked … surprised.

"Who the fuck are you?" the man blurted.

Well, fuck. Charles launched himself across the

room, darting around the edge of the dining table. The guy had no time to prepare, and Charles was savage … angry … he threw himself on the man, his hands on his shoulders, his weight up, in the air, over the height of the man and bringing him down like a big cat on an antelope.

His weight and force forward taking the legs from the guy, the two of them tumbled into the living room, to the floor, where the guy grunted out some weak exclamation as he hit the floor. Wind bursting from him. He breathed in, sounding like a broken vacuum cleaner.

Charles was up. On his knees. He brought his two hands together, fingers clamped in between each other. He threw them up like a hammer and then down onto the man's chest first. Taking even more air from him. He was coughing and choking. Even had a little blood at his mouth—although that was probably only from biting his tongue. Hands went up again, this time dropping hard on the guy's face. He cried out, anguish, more than pain, and Charles crawled up him, knees on his chest. A punch to the face. The guy's head rocked back, bouncing from the carpet.

He reached forward and grabbed at Charles's hands, trying to contain him. Restrain him. Charles slapped his hands away, for a brief second the two of them looking like children slap fighting on the playground.

Charles rolled off, glancing at the man. The driver. It had to be the driver. What the fuck did he do, stay here like *staff*? Fucking hell. She *must* have money.

The driver huffed air in, the noise of an asthmatic moose coming from him. Charles up to his feet. He toe punted the driver in the back as he rolled away, his toes contacting the ribs, near the lungs. He nearly folded himself inside out. Curling like a backwards C, tortured and tormented, distorting himself, his hands clawing at his chest. Breath gone. The ability to *breathe* gone.

Charles hopped, on one foot, massaging his toes on the other. "Cunt," he muttered. He looked quickly around the room. Something quick, and quiet. He hobbled over to the bookcase. Grabbed a copy of a hardback book with the picture of a man in a wheel chair on the front of it. He went to the driver, and when he righted his head, looking upwards, Charles dropped down, from standing with the book up, to his knees. He thrust the book into the driver's face. Smashing it into his mouth. His teeth splitting apart and splintering, blood gushing into his mouth as he looked, stunned, up, by Charles to the ceiling. Charles brought the book up, the driver's lips broken and split. Blood goo-ing out, sticky, holding to the book and creating the mozzarella-like drawbridge between book and mouth. Then he crashed it back down again. Hard. Harder, maybe. His own air starting to struggle into his lungs with the effort. The book ruptured the driver's nose the second time. A large book. Girthy. He smashed it up and down, the driver going from struggling to breathe to stillness, as the corner of the book crumpled his face, it getting easier the more times Charles did it.

As he slowed. Tired.

He slipped from his knees to the side, stopping on his arse, his elbow up on the sofa. Breathing hard. He needed to get more cardio, that was for sure. He looked over the mess that was the driver's face.

"Won't be needing you anymore," he said. "I guess you're fired." There was a splinter of bone sticking from the face. Through the flesh, and out, like a tiny sun dial. With the big light on in the middle of the room, it even cast a shadow into whatever was left of his face.

He was, however, still breathing. One eye was open, but it had been wrecked in Charles's angered onslaught, and he was pretty sure that even if the guy was conscious, he wouldn't be able to see from it.

The other was closed, and he looked … peaceful.

"Fuck," Charles muttered. He pushed himself to his feet and looked at the ceiling. Listening. She must still be up there.

He went back out the door to the dining room and through to the kitchen. Took a blade from the knife block. Big one. Probably had a name. Didn't know what it was. Didn't care much, to be honest.

Back to the driver.

He hadn't moved. Charles was probably going to be doing him a favour. Being fucked up like that. He might make it, pull through, like, but he probably wasn't going to look good ever again. Nor drive. Not being blind in one eye, so what good was there in going on? He got to his knees next to this guy's head.

His stomach acidic and vile. Fucking hell. Not now.

He didn't know the best way to do it. He'd never been in this situation before. He thought about all the films he'd seen. Knife wound to the gut—apparently could kill you instantly, or take days to finish you off, depending on which film you were watching. Slash across the throat? Did it matter where you slashed?

The smell had crept up his nose by then. The smell of iron and copper joining with the acidic taste hiking up his throat. "Fuck," he muttered, again. He took the knife, shaking it in his hand for a moment, and then drew it to the driver's neck. He slit it across the skin like he'd seen done. The blade didn't really do much, to be honest. He expected the flesh to part like the red seas and the blood to gush out forward. Squirting maybe. But the knife barely damaged the flesh. So he started to saw.

He was tired of this before he started.

The blade finally cutting into the meat. Apparently films lied and it did matter which knife you took from the block to do this shit with. Should have gotten a bread knife maybe?

The driver twitched, and Charles lurched back, thinking he was suddenly getting a second wind and he was going to throw himself back into it.

But a small death knell was all he got.

Charles was breathing hard. He dropped the knife down to the carpet. Too late to not make a mess. He looked at the stains on the white flooring. Who the fuck had white carpet? It was fucked. That was for sure. He'd need to pull it all up. Burn it in the back garden, maybe.

And that smell.

He focussed on the driver's gut. It wasn't rising and falling anymore.

Good. Job done.

Chapter 8

Charles sat on the sofa for a moment, getting his breath back. The house was quiet. Maybe she was asleep up there? He looked at the ceiling, studying it, like it might enlighten him.

Then he stood. Checked the curtains in the living room, and turned the TV off. The driver had been watching some horror movie by the looks of it.

His goo had pooled on the carpet, a giant ring now around him. Looked like a red rug. Charles stared at it for a moment. No. There was no way he was going to get around it. He was going to have to replace the carpet. Even if he could pretend it was a rug, there was the smell.

He flipped the lights off as he left the living room. To the front hall and the stairs. Up. He walked slowly, and quietly. The house was warm. Warm all the way around not just the odd room. Properly warm. Like a normal person. *Wait until dad hears about this pad. Eschewing myself in with normal people.* He reached the top, the landing. Even the stairs didn't creak. The hallway was dark at the top, but he used the light coming from downstairs to navigate. To the back of the house. That was where she was going to be. He'd seen. He went to the door and listened.

There was no sound behind it. *Asleep*, he assumed. Taking the door handle, he held it for a few moments, awaiting the rush running through him to quieten. He didn't want to bust into the room and scare her. Not at all. The pink room. His eyes, closed, facing the door. He could see it. The room beyond …

from the videos. It was girly. He liked that about her.

His heart, slowing. He was ready. Ready to take this step.

Charles opened the door and looked in. The room dark with shadows. And pink. Very pink.

He looked at the bed. It was empty.

Blinking a few times, before believing his eyes, Charles looked at the bed. Where the fuck was she? She should have been there. *Had* to have been there. He flipped the light on, more concerned about the lack of Lauren, than anything else.

The light, bright, burned his eyes for a few seconds before he could truly see. Water coming from the left one. The room was, though. Empty. He was smitten by it, just for an instant. Never once thinking the pink room would be this … warm. Inviting.

He turned on his heels. Shit. Maybe she was in the bathroom. He hoped she didn't hear him putting the driver down. He went to the door opposite the pink room. Listened at it. Nothing. Again. The fuck? He opened it. Looked in.

Bathroom. Had all the disabled attachments money could buy, but it was gloomy, and empty.

Frowning, his stomach feeling almost as empty, Charles looked at the last door. She had to be behind that one. He stepped up and opened it without thought. The darkness beyond. He could see her, in the bed. There. Sleeping. A mound of flesh, half under the sheets, half on top. The room was warm. Hot. Moist. It smelt of sex.

"Close the door," she muttered. Turning in the darkness.

Charles realised she was upset by the light, and stepped into the room, closing the door. None of this felt right. Why wasn't she upset that the driver had come into her room at night? Why was she sleeping in there, and not in *her* room?

He stroked his face. Listlessly standing there at the door. In the darkness. Lauren there on the bed before him.

His eyes adjusting to the room, he could see her again. Head on the pillow, looking to the side. One arm up under it. Supporting her head. Her whole leg out the covers, near the bottom. The other, her stump, under them. He wondered if she felt the cold more in that one.

"You getting in or what?"

She sounded half-asleep. More out of it, than not.

Charles cleared his throat, uncomfortable, suddenly. He went around the side of the bed, the other side to her, and pulled his shirt off, over his head. Kicked his shoes off, carefully. Took his trousers down. Then he slipped into the bed next to her, careful not to touch her. He lay there. Head on the pillow. The bed had a faint smell of perfume. Her. It smelled of her. He breathed it in. He had no idea what to expect from that smell. Never really thought about it. You don't do you? Wondering what people are going to smell like. Or maybe that was just him. He stared at the ceiling, pulled the sheet over himself. The warmth bit into him, alien and foreign. Casual warmth.

Money, he supposed.

It was weird not having to put a heater on and warm the room before getting into bed. Even weirder already having a warm body in the bed waiting. He was smiling. Just happened. Smiling. Happiness.

Wow. He had not expected it to happen this quickly at all. He let out a little chuckle. Engorged in the ease.

Then she screamed.

Lauren rolled across the bed, away from him, and flipped the lamp on next to the bed. She sat there. The two of them looking at each other for a split second. Time paused.

Charles thought it the most wonderful second. Then he noticed that the sheets had blood smeared over them from his hands, the room's smell was changing, from the sweetness of her to the far more familiar stink of him. His life. His behaviour.

But it was okay. He could fix that.

"Who are you?" she said, little more than a whisper. Her eyes flicked down him. The bloody sheets fallen away.

She was checking him out. Charles pushed the sheets further back, revealing a little more of himself. "You don't recognise me," he said. "No," he continued, quickly. "Of course you don't. It was a long time ago." Charles suddenly averted his eyes. She was wearing a vest thing. A tank top. A tiny pair of panties below them. He looked down himself. His body dotted with the driver's blood. Hands caked in it. "I'll clean all this up."

She looked from him to the door. "Where's …" the words died in her mouth.

"You don't need him now." Charles smiled. "You have me." He pushed himself from the bed. Stood there. Like he was some statue, a prize, an Oscar.

"We were at school together."

She was looking between him and the door. When he said that, she looked him in the face properly. A slight frown, like the memory was there, but needed to fight through. "Yes," she said. Her voice low and sexy.

Charles rounded the bed, getting to her side, between her and the door. "You get back in," he said. "Stay warm."

She pulled herself back across the bed, staying away from him, pulling the sheet up like a shield. "What do you want?" she asked.

"Just for you to be you. I can help."

Her eyes darted over him. A fixation on his hands. "What happened to Donnie?"

Charles held a look of confusion for a moment, then his eyes brightened. "The driver," he said, "oh, he won't be any bother. I'll clean all that up later."

She stared at him. Her breaths slow and shallow. Then she lowered the sheet a little. Like she was relaxing. "Science," she said.

She *was* remembering. Charles straightened. "Yep," he chirped. He must have made an impact. That was something. He thought she looked peaky though. "You want anything from downstairs?"

She shook her head. "I'm fine."

"Yes you are." He winked at her. Then stopped himself. Maybe this wasn't the time for cheeky chappie play. He backed himself to the door. Unsure of what to do next. "Well, shall we turn in?"

Lauren just blinked at him.

Charles came back around the bed and looked at

the bloody sheets. "Fuck," he muttered. He bent forward and took them in fistfuls before pulling them hard, from the bed, from Lauren's grip. He pulled them into himself and rolled them around like a toilet roll. She let out a little *eep*, and retreated as far up the bed as she could. "Where are the clean ones?" he asked.

She pointed. To the door. Out to the hall.

"And?" he said.

"The cupboard on the landing."

Charles raised his eyebrows in acknowledgement and fumbled the door open. He stepped out. Tossed the sheets to a pile at the top of the stairs. Then looked around for the light switch. Now she was up, he didn't need to creep around in the dark, did he? Lights on, he stalked back across the bedroom door.

Lauren was on the bed, had her phone in her hand. She looked at him, full of fear.

What the fuck? This wasn't going right at all. He strode into the bedroom and snatched the phone from her. "I can look after you," he said. He threw the phone across the bedroom, the plastic shattering on the wall opposite. She screamed, hands up to her face to protect her. Crying.

"Hey, hey, hey," he said. Crawling up on the bed. He tried to pull her arms away from her face, and hold her, but she struck out at him, hands curled to fists. He held her wrists and waited for the fight to go, before he looked down at her. "What's your fucking problem?" he snapped.

She wouldn't look at him.

"Fuck," he said. He let her go, dropping to the bed, before going to the hallway and getting the clean sheets from the cupboard. Huge fucking cupboard. Fuck it. This place put his hovel to shame. He looked up into the cupboard. Probably used to house the immersion heater. He returned to the bedroom, where she hadn't moved. "So why are you sleeping in here tonight?" he asked, dropping sheets to the bed.

She shook her head, seemingly unable to speak.

"Just put these on the bed, right?" he said. "Or do you want to sleep in the pink room?"

"What?" she said. At least that was what he thought she said, through the grizzle face.

Charles sighed. "Fucking hell. The pink room? You wanna sleep in there?"

The penny looked to finally drop and she shook her head, got herself from the bed, and pulled the sheets around. Half-heartedly, in Charles opinion. He crawled over the bed. Over towards her. She tried to retreat, but there was nowhere to go.

Charles got close. He put his hand out, slowly, like he was about to pet the dog of a stranger, trying to show he wasn't a threat, but equally, to show he was going to touch her. She watched his hand. Striped in blood. He had to admit, it wasn't a good look, not really. "It's okay," he said. Finally, reaching her skin. "I won't hurt you." He smiled. It was as warm as he could make it.

The drying blood on his face, cracking as he did.

"What do you want?" she whispered. She was trying. That was nice.

Charles felt a little bolder. She was clearly attracted to him, and that was good. All in good time. But he bravely moved his flesh over hers, reaching the knee of her complete leg first. He rolled his hand around it, feeling her heat. She imbued a warmth that he didn't have, but he dismissed it as just the cold weather outside. Settling into him.

Hard to shake.

He pulled himself a little closer, his hand moving to her stump. He stroked it gently. His body responding to her closeness. He didn't mean for it to happen, and certainly wasn't expecting it. But she was hot. Half naked. She was watching him, shuddering lightly under his touch. Shaking with excitement.

"You want me?" she said.

Charles looked down himself. His cock protruding within his shorts. Visible and obvious. "Shit," he muttered. He curled himself over. Hoping she couldn't see it.

"It's okay," she said.

Charles eyes slipped up to hers, drawing hers back to his. She looked around the room, quickly, but her look always returned to him.

"You like me, right?" she asked.

Charles nodded like a dog. "Yes," he said, breathing the word out.

"So why don't you take a shower. Clean yourself up for me. You want me in the pink room? I can be waiting in there for you."

He was still nodding. "That works." He pushed himself from the bed. Getting to the door before stopping. He looked back at her. "Who was he?" he asked. There was something that didn't feel right.

"Who?" she asked, her look, that of innocence.

Something wasn't right at all. "Him," he barked.

His finger pointing down, to the floor, to the ground floor. The person downstairs. *The corpse.*

"My …" she paused. "… driver," she said. A small smile.

Charles didn't move from the spot. He just stared at her.

"What?"

She was lying to him. Trying to get him out the room. He shook his head. "I can take care of you. I don't think you understand."

"I do. You go and shower and I'll wait for you in the pink room. We can be … together." She swallowed after the word came out. "That's what you want, isn't it? You want me."

Charles shook his head. "What? No. I want to be … you," he said. Hold on. That sounded worse somehow. "Sure, I want us to have a complete relationship." He smiled, almost shyly looking away. "But more than that. I want to be like you. So we can balance."

CHAPTER 9

Lauren shook her head. "I don't understand."

Charles shook his, but like he was shaking out the cobwebs. He returned to the bed, excited to try and tell her. "No. I want to be *like* you." He touched her stump. The emphasis on the word *like*.

She looked like she had physically stopped herself from withdrawing. "I ... I—" Her face showed nothing but confusion. Eyes darting about.

He showed her his leg. "Like yours." He made a sawing motion.

She swallowed, blinking.

"But you're right. I do need to shower." He looked around the room quickly. Then climbed from the bed. Pulled open the bedside cabinet. A dildo rolled to the front of the drawer. Packet of condoms. Lube. He looked at the items for a moment, then over at her. His face somewhere between a disgruntled father and a horny fan. His faces fought for supremacy for a moment, and then a smile. "Naughty girl," he said. He looked at her. His eyes moving to the second bedside cabinet. Something dropped in his mind. A penny.

"You're fucking the driver," he said.

She shook her head, violently from side to side. "No," she said. "No."

He was nodding in time with her protestations. "You fucking ..." Charles stopped himself from saying *whore*. It wasn't polite. "Fuck." He rounded the bed, as she pushed herself away, again, to the other side. Trying to keep space between them. He opened the other drawer. A sports mag and a watch. Letters, pushed in. A *man drawer*. "Fuck." He bent forward opened the next drawer. Metal. Fucking cuffs. He swiped them. Took them from the drawer and showed them to her. "You've been fucking him. For what? Fucking free lifts?"

She screamed. "No. Donnie's not my driver."

But it was too late. Charles was around the bed. Hand up, he slapped the back of his hand across her cheek, knocking her to the side. She over balanced and sprawled to the bed. Her hand clasping the side of her face. He grabbed her by the wrist and yanked her straight, on the bed. Used the cuffs to cuff her to the headboard. One hand above her head, and then he stopped. Looked down her. He wanted to … what the fuck did he want? Fucking … the driver. "Wait there," Charles blurted.

He stormed to the bathroom. The door left open. He turned the shower on. Hot water instantly flooding from it. Charles pulled his shorts off and stepped in under the water. The clear liquid rushing over him, the blood dissipating into it. He hung his head forward, eyes closed. She didn't *mean* anything. Of course she didn't. She just needed to remember who he was properly. And you can't blame her for fucking the driver. Everyone needed to fuck sometimes, right? Maybe that was why she kept asking Charles if he wanted her. Maybe she was looking for some action?

He opened his eyes and looked down at his cock, water trickling from the end of it like a cherub fountain.

Shit. He'd misread the signs. She wanted to fuck and he was only thinking about himself and what he wanted. He grabbed the shower gel from the side and squirted it into his hand. It had a footballer on the front and a name like *Bear Punch* or something, so it must have been the drivers.

She was fucking him, so he couldn't have smelled bad, could he? Charles washed the soap over his body. Made sure the blood was gone. Probably a turn off. He paid special attention to his cock. Made sure that was clean. He was going to need to shower again after, probably.

Then he turned the shower off. Stood there. Basking in the steam of the room. The warmth. His legs had turned from the red of the cold back to their normal colour. He heard something. Out in the hall. He turned and got to the door of the bathroom in time to see her.

She was standing on one leg (obviously) and was halfway to the top of the stairs. To the stair lift. She looked back at him. Fear in her eyes. She was leaving. Running for it. She thought he was only able to think of himself over her. It was all a misunderstanding.

He ran along the corridor towards her. She had a crutch under one arm. The other hand was out on the wall, easily unlocked sex-cuffs still attached at the wrist. The wall was white, apart from the smears of blood that were there from him, from when he came up. Unseen in the darkness.

Shit. He was going to have to decorate as well as re-carpet, wasn't he?

He grabbed at her, but she swung the crutch at him. It caught him, naked as he was, in the ribs, a shock, stinging pain blossomed in his torso and he cried out. Losing his balance, the two of them crashing together.

Over the discarded sheets. Down.

The stairs. The rails of the stair lift. The two of them tumbling over each other.

Charles saw the flash of skin. Her clothes. His skin. His head bounced off the stair lift rail. A flash of light, stronger than lightning, sparks in his eyes. He suddenly stopped. He was laying flat. Must have reached the bottom of the stairs.

And he was still breathing. That was something.

He could feel heat in his head, a pulse thudding there. Warmth spreading. He tried to move his arms, but they were so heavy. He just wanted to reach up and see if he was bleeding. Yet even that seemed beyond his control.

So he lay there. She was there too. Next to him. She wasn't moving. "Hey," he said. "Babe." He lifted his head, just an inch and the world swam, the walls spinning around, waves of nausea crashing over him.

Sickness in his stomach.

His head dropped back to the floor. The blackness surrounding him. Creeping in from the edge of his vision, in deeper. Like he was sinking. He couldn't stop it. Couldn't fight the ocean that took him down.

CHAPTER 10

Charles opened his eyes. The ceiling above him. He was cold. Felt so cold. He was on the floor, right? Naked. With Lauren. *Fuck.* Lauren. She might be hurt. "Hey," he said. He tried to move his head but couldn't. That was worse. He was sure he could move his head before. When they …. They went down the stairs. "Lauren?" He waited. Breathing was hard. Like he'd had the wind knocked out of him. "Are you okay?"

"I'm fine," she said. "Bump on my head, is all."

"Thank fuck," Charles said, relaxing back a little. "I thought you were hurt."

"I'm fine," she echoed.

"Where are you?"

She came into view above him. Standing over him, but not like he was on the floor.

"Where am I?" Charles looked around but he couldn't see shit. Not a single identifying feature.

"You're still at mine. Ours, I suppose," she said. "As you live here now."

Charles tried to nod. Couldn't even do that. "I live here now," he repeated. She'd accepted him. That was good. No. Better than good. Wonderful. "Why can't I move?"

"You fell down the stairs," she said. "You fell down the stairs and knocked your head. There was a lot of blood. I wondered if you might not make it, like if you'd really hurt yourself. But I bandaged you up." Her voice was unwavering. Monotone.

"Thank you," he said. "But I can't move."

"No." Then she left his view.

Charles pulled on his arms. He could feel something digging into them. Something hard. He couldn't feel the same on his legs. Just a warmth that was spreading down there. "What's going on?"

"You can't feel that?"

"What?"

"Oh, you are a naughty boy. But ..." she came back into view and smiled down at him. "You may have hurt yourself more badly than I thought."

"What?" Charles hissed.

"You peed yourself," She said. Disappearing again.

All the coming and going was starting to scare Charles. Just a little. She said he lived there now. That was good. But he couldn't feel that he'd pissed himself. "What have you done?"

"I have done nothing," she said. "It looks like you're the one who's done something."

"I don't understand." He pulled at the straps or binds or whatever he had around his wrists and hands. Tried to turn and twist. Something wasn't right. He couldn't feel everything like normal. "What's happened to me?" he asked. His voice twisted a little in fear. There was something badly wrong. She'd done something to him.

She appeared at his face again. Calm and serene. "You did fall badly. But I'm taking no chances."

Gone again.

Charles looked around wildly. Where had she gone? What was she going to do? He couldn't feel his feet. He must have been laying on them. Or maybe she'd strapped him down too hard and they'd fallen asleep. "Please," he whispered. "Let me go. I won't say anything."

She laughed. "You won't say anything?" she echoed. "You won't say anything. You won't say anything." She came back up.

He wished he could move his head, and see what she was doing.

"You fuck. You fucking cunt." She spat as the words escaped her. "You won't say anything. After what you did to my boyfriend? I found him lying in a pool of his own …" She growled out and was gone again. "Can you feel this?" she asked.

Charles whined. "What?" There was a feeling of movement down his body somewhere. But nothing else. Maybe his limbs *had* fallen asleep. Maybe she'd drugged him. Like in that film. Some local anaesthetic. Make him think there was something wrong with him. She slipped up again. She had a fleck of blood on her face. Smiling.

"Can't feel anything at all, can you?"

Charles felt a tear roll down his face. He couldn't. He couldn't feel *anything* she was doing. "What have you done?" he asked.

She reached up and did something to the side of his head and suddenly he could move it. He instinctively looked up to his hands. They were tied off with para-cord to whatever he was on. He followed it around. Looked like a table of some sort. She'd removed a strap or something from his head. That was why he could move it now. He continued to look out, further. He was in the basement. There were beams over his head. Cobwebs. Now he could move better, he raised his head, and looked down his body.

There was a knife sticking from his leg. It looked like it was an inch or two into the flesh, deep enough that it was holding its own weight up like Gordon fucking Ramsey had jammed it in there. "What have you done to me?" he asked. He couldn't stop his mind from swirling, rolling. Tail spinning. "Why can't I … why doesn't that …?"

"Hurt?" she said.

His eyes flickered from the knife to her. She was standing there. A couple of feet from the table. A crutch under one arm.

"Looks like you broke something in there," she said. "I've looked online and it suggests that you have damage to your spinal column from a fall or trauma." She smiled like a cat that got the cream. Coming to him. "I'm going to call the police now, and report the break in. My boyfriend. He's been killed by some lunatic." Then she pulled a syringe.

Charles hadn't even seen it.

"You know," she said, her calmness disconcerting. "It's amazing the drugs they give you when you've lost a limb in an accident. They never ask for them back, either."

She stuck it in his upper arm. Plunger down.

Charles yelped out at the stinging pain, and then the room started to spin. Slowly. Not like he was getting seasick or anything. Just a gentle roll. A euphoria washing over him. His head rocking back to the table. He stared at the ceiling. It was delightful. A most wonderful sensation. He wondered what it was. He needed to get hold of some.

The darkness, the shadowed corners of the room moved. Crept out towards him like a shade made of demons, moving unseen. Black creeping death, towards him.

"Wait," he called out. At least, he thought he did. "No." He looked around the spirits of night to her, moving away, towards the stairs. Clonk, pause, clonk. The sound of her wooden leg. Extra one. Then it was gone. He tried to lift his head, but he couldn't see her.

The blackness surrounding him. Inside him. Taking him to another place. Somewhere cold.

Lonely.

CHAPTER 11

Sickness washed over Charles' consciousness immediately he awoke. Sickness and weakness. His mouth so dry his lips clagging together. Tongue stuck to the top of his mouth. He opened it a little, feeling the skin clinging on to stay closed. Opened his eyes, before shutting them again. He willed some words to his mouth, but they escaped him only as a wheeze. His brain slowly turning.

Where was he?

He remembered being in the house. Then the basement. That was right. Then the demons. He dragged his eyes open, sore and dry, and lifted his head only an inch. The feeling of an extra pint of blood lolling in his head. At the back. "What?" This time the word did come from him. Pathetic and shallow. He rested back. His head laying on something hard, and the feeling of the liquid sitting in it, heavy and pregnant. The worst hangover of all time. He blinked a few times. Wettened his eyeballs. Felt them better in his head than before. Tried to move. He was numb. All over. Just a feeling in his fingers.

Freezing cold.

"Awake."

The voice came from everywhere, breaking the silence.

"Good. I thought I'd fucked it up and given you too much."

Lauren's face, there above his.

"I thought you might have been in a coma." She smiled down on him. "You'll be pleased to know that the DNA you left behind was enough for the police to identify you as the intruder. Charles, isn't it? I really don't remember," she said. "I heard you were in school with me." She looked in his eyes with pity in hers. "You clearly meant nothing to me."

Then she was gone.

"So you're wanted for murder. Amongst other things. They seemed surprised that I wanted to stay in the house. After all that. Thought I might want to stay with family until after they'd caught you. They said it was probably a coincidence that we were at school together, but that they couldn't rule anything out."

Back again.

"You might come back, apparently." A smile. "But they're never going to find you. Are they?"

"What do you want?" he said, breathing the word out into the room.

"I want Donnie back," she said. She didn't have malice behind the words. She didn't have anything behind the words. She just let them out from her.

Charles lifted his head and looked down his body. He was naked. His legs weren't strapped down. He tried to move. Seeing his chance to break free, but they did nothing. His head, knocking on the table that his hands were strapped to, as he dropped it back.

"I even cleaned the shit off you this morning," she said. "Don't want you getting an infection now, do we?"

"No," he wheezed.

"So," she said. "I've done some research." She

smiled at him as he watched, unable to move. "And we'll see what we can do, 'kay?"

She fiddled with something that Charles couldn't identify, no matter how much he strained. Head up. She had something metal. Several things. She was picking them up, admiring them, and then putting them down. She seemed to settle on one and she came back to the table. She struggled a little, holding a blade, and using a crutch. She was wearing white. A lab coat. Like at school. She saw him looking and then glanced down herself. "I thought it fitting," she said. Then she stabbed the blade into his leg.

Charles screamed. "No. Please." But he couldn't *feel* it. Like it was someone else's leg. "Oh, God."

"He won't help you now," she said, absently. "According to the videos, I have to be careful that I don't nick an artery before I'm ready to clamp."

Charles watched blood flowing from his limb. Gushing out. So much of it. How could she be doing this? He felt the hot of his tears as he watched her slide the scalpel around his leg. Pulling the skin back, revealing the flesh. The table beneath sodden in his blood. He saw piss dribbling without control from his flaccid cock. Mixing with the blood on the table below. He was struggling to breathe. His breaths coming short and sharp. Panic. She glanced up at him, perhaps concerned that he might be about to die, before ignoring him with a little smile and getting back to her work.

Slicing through his muscles and tendons, working her way to the bone like he was a chicken.

He screamed. Yowled. Incomprehensible growls escaping him as he pushed and pulled his hands the only part of him that still seemed to work. But he shivered and he shuddered.

She clamped down on the artery. Closing off the blood supply to the rest of the body. A glance to him, and she pulled a face, like she was on a roller coaster. "Big moment," she said. Then she cut through the artery, and stopped. Frozen. Watching. Waiting.

Nothing happened.

Charles' head thumped. He could see the demons surrounding him again. Blackness coming.

"All good," she said.

Charles dropped his head back to the table and looked at the ceiling. He was waiting for death now. Then he noticed a camera. In the ceiling. He was sure it wasn't there before. He looked to the side. Another. The basement, littered with cameras. Filming this. Filming her, removing his leg. He weakly lifted his head. She had a bone saw in her hand. The flesh stripped back, the white of the bone visible. She dropped the teeth to the white, and drew it back. Pushed forward. The juddering of the metal on bone shaking his whole body.

The demons close.

The blackness right there.

CHAPTER 12

Charles awoke. Opened his eyes. The basement again. He could see a drip to his side. The whole room was a blur. His eyes not working correctly. When he tried to speak, nothing more than the yell of an animal came out. He rolled his head around, blinking time and again. There was a smell. A terrible, terrible smell. It was like a butchers shop in the middle of summer, along with a public toilet. Shit and piss and copper, along with mould and rot. Warm flesh. He raised his head, to look to where the vague memory was. That thing she was doing. His leg. It was a stump, shortly above the knee. Yellow putrid pus hung from the poorly wrapped bandages. He cried. Head dropping down. Still couldn't feel anything but exhaustion and vile sickness in his gut.

He shivered but felt the beads of sweat on him move as he did.

He lay there. Wasn't sure for how long. Charles wasn't even sure if he'd blacked out again or not. He just focussed on getting his eyes working properly. Trying to get his mouth to form words.

There was a noise eventually. Cutting through the silence of the basement.

Clonk.

He looked around. Unable to see how she was getting into the room. But she was there.

"You stink like a trash pile." She came to his side. "Not long now, I fear. I was hoping that I'd have more time, but I don't think I've done a good job. You have a constant fever and don't look, but maggots, too. I think." She looked around. "Not as sterile in here as I hoped, I guess."

Charles breathed slow. It was hard. He wanted to scream and shout and cry, but the strength wasn't there.

"I guess you're never going to … what was it you said … balance? Balance with me." She rounded the table for the first time standing on his left side. Next to his still whole leg. "Guess nothing matters, now, right?" She was wearing old decorating clothes. Fucked and stained. She had a scalpel—*the* scalpel—clotted in dry blood in her hand. Already poking half-heartedly at his leg. Like cutting this one off was barely worth the trouble.

Charles scanned around the cameras. Red lights flickering and flashing. Even if she wasn't that interested she was still recording it. "What are you making?" he said. The words came out gnarled and dry. "A film?"

"Well," she replied, never taking her eyes from his leg. "You know me. Anything for the camera. I might keep this for posterity, or maybe see if I can find a buyer on the internet somewhere. Make us *dark web* famous." She giggled, then made a noise like a shit ghost.

Charles raised his head. She was already digging in his numb leg. Blood squitting out to join the rest of the fluids on the table. The patter of them as they slipped to the floor.

The stink of fresh blood joining the cacophony of other smells in the room. "No," he said. "Please don't."

But she didn't reply. And she just worked. The

flesh being hacked through, no care or precision this time. The bone saw coming out while there was still flesh there.

Charles blacked out on more than one occasion, the demons taking him for minutes, then waking him again, just to make him watch. Taking his eyes from what she was doing he looked instead at Lauren. She was sad. Looking like she was working a line job in a factory. Tired and bored.

She still had clamped the artery, though, and still Charles lived.

CHAPTER 13

Charles tried to open his eyes. It was hard. Something clagged them together. Crusty and dry. He tried to move his arm, bring his hand down to his face, forgetting in his half-conscious stupor. Finally, managing to pull them open. He could see the beams with one eye. The other blurred. He wasn't sure if there was something in it. Or over it. But it stung. The drip was empty next to him. Head thumping.

He managed to raise his head to look. The leg gone. He now had two dead stumps. All he could smell was rotten flesh and death.

The demons in the basement, crawling around him. What little sight he did have a tunnel of blackness, like he was looking at everything down a tube. They were watching him. Waiting for him.

Waiting for his death.

He rested his head back, banging it on the table. He hadn't expected the demons to come for him so soon.

Shutting his eyes, he took the moments to think. He wondered if his dad believed the police, when they had inevitably gone to him to try and get a lead on Charles. Of course he would.

He opened his eye. Light.

Bright light. In his face. His open eye looking, the other now not moving. Someone was with him.

"You are still alive, I see." Lauren. "I thought I'd lost you again."

Charles looked around. Eye stinging, dry. Coated

over in some gelatinous goo. He must have blacked out again. He wished he knew how long he'd been there. He tried to speak, but there was something wrong. It was as if everything in his mouth was made of sand. Everything he could *feel,* hurt.

"According to Google, the infection will take you eventually." She squeezed the drip. "But dehydration will take you quicker." She looked down into his good (er) eye. "You look terrible." She smiled, and brought up a tablet. Showed him this video feed. It was of something gross. A swamp of fluids. Bile. Shit. Something in there moved.

It was him.

What was left of him.

He closed his eye and wished he could cry. He wished the demons would take him. Hell had to be better than this. Anything had to be. But when he got there he was going to wait for her, because she was going to get there eventually, too. He smiled in his head. Atrophy and dehydration stopping his physical movement.

"But I still want to know if I can do it," she said.

He didn't look. Didn't care what she was talking about.

But he could feel her. She was touching his arm. Eye opened. What now? What was she doing? She stroked his skin, and just the touch brought soreness and pain. In desperation, determined to speak, his mouth moved, but nothing came out. Just shallow breaths and air.

"Aw," she said. "It tried to speak."

Then pain flooded Charles body. Pain like he'd never known. Everything was on fire. Stabbing him.

He looked up to her. She was at his side. The dirty blade in his arm. Hacking at it. Blood drooling slow and thick from it.

He didn't think his blood looked right. But he could barely comprehend the sight, with the pain riding him like a whore. Didn't she know he could feel that?

Didn't she care?

He looked away. With no way to stop her. Or plead. Beg. Or die. He just hoped that the demons would take him. Let him ride out this journey bathed in the warmth of sleep.

And they did.

Charles couldn't open his eye. He lay. Lost. He could feel a freeness in his shoulders. His arms gone. Nothing below the belt. He didn't know if there was anything there to feel. Or just a nothingness.

What she'd cut from him was a mystery.

But blind and mute he had time to think. Fleeting moments between an unconscious blackness, and a conscious one. Not being able to tell waking moments from those of slumber, no passage of time, he wondered if she still watched him. His tormented broken body. If she filmed him. So he could be famous.

Like she was.

And how soon the demons would come and take him.

Or if this was already Hell.

About the Author

Ash is a British horror author. He resides in the south, in the Garden of England. He writes horror that is sometimes fantastical, sometimes grounded, but always deeply graphic, and black with humour.

www.ashericmore.com

Printed in Great Britain
by Amazon